The Smurfs and the Miller

by Peyo and Matagne

Random House 🏠 New York

First American Edition, 1984.
English text copyright © 1984 by Peyo. All rights reserved under International and Pan-American Copyright Conventions. Published in the United States by Random House, Inc., New York, and simultaneously in Canada by Random House of Canada Limited, Toronto. Originally published in Belgium as *Le moulin des schtroumpfs* by Dupuis, Marcinelle-Charleroi, 1967.

Library of Congress Cataloging in Publication Data: Peyo. The Smurfs and the miller. Translation of: Le moulin des Schtroumpfs. SUMMARY: The Smurfs help an honest miller whose mill has been bewitched by the evil wizard Gargamel. [1. Millers—Fiction. 2. Magic—Fiction] I. Matagne, Michel. II. Title PZ7.P44818Sr 1984 [E] 83-3302 ISBN: 0-394-86076-4
Manufactured in the United States of America

1 2 3 4 5 6 7 8 9 0

SMURF is a trademark of SEPP International S.A.

Once upon a time, in a land not very far from the village of the Smurfs, there was a kind and honest miller who worked hard every day. From all over the country, farmers brought their sacks of grain to be ground into flour. The next day, when they came back to get the freshly milled flour, the miller would weigh the sacks and the farmers would gladly pay him for his work.

One fine day a new visitor came to the mill: the wicked wizard Gargamel.

"Listen, miller," said Gargamel, "I want to make a deal with you. I have invented a magic powder that makes flour heavier. If you add a pinch of this powder to a sack half filled with flour, it will weigh as much as a sack full of regular flour.

"Use my magic powder," said Gargamel. "Then you can keep half of the farmers' flour for yourself, and we'll share the profits. What do you say?"

"Never!" the miller shouted angrily. "I will not cheat the farmers!" And he chased Gargamel away.

The wizard shook his fist and shouted back, "You'll be sorry, miller! I'll get my revenge on you soon!"

That night Gargamel crept back to the mill. In the pale, silent light of the moon, he painted a mysterious sign on the stone wall.

"This evil spell will teach that miller a lesson!" cackled Gargamel.

The next day the Smurfs set off to visit their friend the miller. They carried their sacks of grain to be ground, and as they walked they sang a happy, smurfy song.

"Just think of all the cakes we can smurf from the flour!" said Greedy Smurf.

"I hate flour," said Grouchy Smurf. But he walked on anyway.

But when the Smurfs came to the mill, they stopped singing. The miller was standing at his door with a sad look on his face.

"There is a spell on my mill!" the good man explained. "Last night someone painted this sign on the wall and now the mill is bewitched!"

"Bewitched? How?" asked Papa Smurf.

"Come and see," said the miller. And all the Smurfs followed him into the mill.

The miller took a sack filled with forty pounds of grain and poured it into the hopper. The grindstones crushed the grain and a sifter sorted out the flour from the grains' shells. Then the miller went downstairs and gathered the flour—but there were only two pounds!

"Do you see that?" the miller said to the Smurfs. "Most of the grain vanishes into thin air between the grindstones! I start out with forty pounds and end up with two!"

"Maybe there's a hole somewhere and the grain smurfed through it," suggested a Smurf.

"No, no, I checked everything," said the miller. "Oh, dear! What will happen to me? The farmers left their sacks of grain here and tomorrow they'll come to get their flour! They'll never believe what happened. They'll think I cheated them!"

"Wait," said Papa Smurf. "Let's try to get rid of this magic sign that's bewitching your mill."

Papa Smurf rubbed at the sign. The other Smurfs also tried to scrape off the paint. But it was all in vain.

"This must be magic paint," said Papa Smurf. "It won't come off. Nothing can break the spell on the mill, unless—"

Papa Smurf suddenly had an idea! He called to all the little Smurfs and whispered his plan to them. Then he said to the miller, "We're going to smurf an experiment. I can't promise that it will work, but it's worth trying."

"If you could help me, I don't know how I could thank you," said the miller. "But please try!"

The Smurfs immediately set to work. They were little enough to slip among the big wooden gears of the mill. Led by Papa Smurf, they scurried about, slashing, cutting, sawing, bolting.

When they were finished, Papa Smurf said to the miller, "Now, grind a new sack of grain."

"But won't that grain also disappear?" asked the miller.

"Try and see," Papa Smurf said with a smile.

The miller took another forty-pound sack of grain and poured it into the hopper. Then he went downstairs to collect the flour. It was amazing! The sack was filled in the wink of an eye, and the miller quickly had to place a second one in front of the opening. It filled up just as quickly, and then another, and still another!

After the miller had filled twenty sacks, Papa Smurf explained what the Smurfs had done. "We couldn't get rid of the spell, so we reversed it! We made the mill's gears turn in the opposite direction. Instead of getting only a pinch of flour from a pound of grain, you'll now get many sackfuls!"

"Thank you, thank you!" exclaimed the miller gratefully. "When the farmers come here tomorrow, I'll have their flour ready!"

The next day Gargamel also came back to the mill. He couldn't wait to see what kind of trouble his evil spell had caused! But what he saw was a crowd of happy farmers leaving the mill, carrying full sacks of flour.

"But what's happened?" Gargamel muttered. "Why is everyone so happy? I must get to the bottom of this!" And he began to make his way toward the mill.

When the Smurfs saw the wizard coming, they said, "It must have been that evil Gargamel who cast the spell! We're going to give him what he deserves!"

And leaning out of a window, the Smurfs dumped a large sack of flour right on Gargamel's head!

Sneezing, coughing, sputtering, and waving his fist, Gargamel ran away as fast as he could. The miller and the Smurfs had a good laugh as they watched him running down the hill.

And now, whenever the Smurfs bring their grain to the mill for grinding, the miller never makes them pay for it.